# Foreword

Three years ago, when I first selected stories for this book, I was amazed at the quality of the entries. Not any more. I now know, from past experience and from visiting dozens of schools all over Britain and further afield, that the pool of young talent is deep, wide and wonderfully rich. And if you think I'm saying that just to be polite, skip this foreword and start reading the stories and poems themselves….

The World Book Day / Evans Short Stories Competition goes from strength to strength. This year we had more entries than ever and the standard keeps climbing. I offer all who entered, especially those whose work is included here, my most sincere congratulations.

As in previous years, it has not been possible to print as many entries as we would have wished. We began the selection process by making a shortlist of 60 from the submissions in the under-12 age group. I then had the unenviable task of selecting two or three pieces beginning with each of the six opening lines, producing the final 16 printed here.

The stories included are by no means the 'best'. That would be an impossible claim. Writing and reading are very personal experiences, so the writing in this book is simply my selection, the entries I liked best. I have also tried to offer a cross-section of ages and regions.

How did I make my choice? Obviously all shortlisted entries stuck to the rules and were well enough punctuated for me to understand what they were trying to say. (I confess to being a bit of a stickler for punctuation: clear punctuation usually shows that a writer is thinking of the reader as they write.) After that I went for originality, fresh and exciting language, and short stories as opposed to mini-novels.

One piece of advice? Whatever the SATs examiners may want, good writing does not mean sentences clogged with unnecessary adjectives, adverbs, clauses and so on. If in doubt, cut it out!

Which means it's time to stop. Thank you for sharing your talent with me and well done, everyone.

**Stewart Ross**
**Blean, 2010**

# LORD OF THE RING DOUGHNUTS

### and other

## stories and poems

#### selected by
#### Stewart Ross

An anthology of winning stories from the 2009-2010
World Book Day Short Stories competition

In association

VISIT OUR WEBSITE
www.evansbooks.co.uk

Published in 2010 by Evans Brothers Limited
2A Portman Mansions
Chiltern Street
London W1U 6NR

British Library Cataloguing in Publication Data
A catalogue record for this book is available from the
British Library

ISBN: 9780237541286

Editor: Bryony Jones
Designers:
Rebecca Fox, Evans
Jo Kennedy, Us2Design

# Acknowledgements

The 2009-2010 World Book Day Short Stories Competition has seen more schools registering and more entries than ever before. A huge thank you to every teacher and librarian for encouraging their students to enter and to every student for writing or illustrating a story or poem.

The entries we received were of an exceptional standard, with winners across the two age categories ranging from five to 17 years old. The new poetry aspect of the competition really captured students' imaginations and helped the competition to grow and continue to go from strength to strength.

Congratulations to the worthy winners and commiserations to those that didn't win. Don't lose heart, remember that even the most successful authors weren't published on their first attempt. We appreciate the hard work and creative effort that goes into every student's entry.

A special thank you is due to all the authors who provided opening lines, and to their publishers. And to Stewart Ross, who once again took on the difficult and unenviable role of judging the competition, and without whom this competition would be an impossible task.

For all their hard work in helping to organise the competition, thanks go to Cathy

Schofield of World Book Day, Truda Spruyt of Colman Getty and Jo Kennedy of US2 for the fantastic cover designs.

Keep an eye on <u>www.worldbookday.com</u> and <u>www.evansbooks.co.uk</u> for information about the next World Book Day Short Stories Competition.

Thanks
Evans Books

# Contents

Ghostly Images Haidee Sticpewich 11

Mystery in the Night Hannah James 15

Lord of the Ring Doughnuts Daniel Knuckle 19

Raspberry The Red Cat Amy Penrose 27

My Father Christopher Barnes 31

Who Poked Me? Maia Lambert 39

Who's There? Louisa Ashdown 41

Down the Hole Jasmine Thirkell 45

Oh No, My Helmet! Greg Susevee 49

The Bookseller Harry Carter 55

Behind the Sign Georgina Evans 61

Vikings Come to Dublin Eleanor Moloney 69

The Attack of the Vikings William O'Hara 71

The Garbage Monster Katrina Harris 77

The Garbage Monster Jake Wood 78

The Garbage Monster Evie O'Neill 79

'That night a mysterious tapping on his bedroom window just wouldn't stop; he had to see what it was.'

Anthony Browne

# Ghostly Images

by Haidee Sticpewich

**That night a mysterious tapping on his bedroom window just wouldn't stop; he had to see what it was.** Edward pushed back the patchwork quilt, and silently crept down the sturdy ladder which led to the royal blue carpet of his bedroom floor. He felt around for his torch for a while, and when Edward found it, he shuffled slowly towards what he thought was the door. Again, Edward felt around for something, this time the brass knob. He turned around to look at the dark silhouette of his sister, sleeping in the bottom bunk.

'I wish you would come with me, Corrie,' Edward murmured.

In reply, he only got a few quiet snores. Edward put a hand to his mouth to muffle his giggles. Then he opened the door, hoping it would not creak and wake his mum and dad up, and his sister. Luckily it didn't. Sighing with relief, Edward made his way along the wide, dark corridor. Looking around him, Edward saw huge, looming shadows cast against the wall. He shivered, clenching his knuckles so tightly that they went white. At last Edward reached the big, open landing. All his muscles in his body relaxed. He started to trudge down the wide steps; they were warm, and the soft, furry, rich purple carpet soothed Edward's tense nerves.

Questions floated around in his head, like, why couldn't I have just looked out of the window, why am I going downstairs, and, why couldn't I have just gone and told Mum and Dad that something was tapping on my window which wouldn't go away?

He soon reached the bolted, thick, wooden door, with a little carving on the edges. The iron door handle curved at the end in an elegant way. Edward slipped on his sister's dark green Crocs. They were cold and somehow awkward on his small feet. Anyway, he thought, Corrie has got bigger feet and she is older than me. Edward quickly unbolted and opened the big, brown door.

Cold wind hit him like a blast in the face, whistling in his freezing, red ears. It was pitch dark and Edward pulled his torch out of his pocket. Blurry figures swooped around each other, some were sinister but beautiful ladies in frilly, decorative ball gowns, some were old sailors or pirates with patches over their eyes and hats with a feather or two stuck in them, and some were princes dressed in lace collared coats embroidered with jewels and wearing highly polished boots. Ghosts, he thought.

Edward just stood there amazed, rooted to the spot. He had never believed there were such things as ghosts, but yes, he had heard stories that ghosts only came out on Halloween and haunted people, not really in a bad way, all they did was scare their victim, that was all....

*I should have known, it's Halloween and they only haunt people who don't believe in them!* he thought. *So that's what was tapping on the window, them!*

Edward quickly stepped backwards and into the house, then he shook the ghosts out of his mind as if they were just annoying flies buzzing around him. He closed the door and bolted it securely, vowing to himself that he would never set foot outside the house if it was a Halloween night. Never. Edward stooped down to take off the Crocs, and then softly padded up the stairs. Edward opened his bedroom door and ran across the room to the bunk bed. He scampered up the ladder, and was soon lying sound asleep in his warm, comforting bed.

Outside, you could just see distant blurry white figures floating away into the blood-red horizon. Soon they were swallowed up by the rising sun.

**Haidee Sticpewich, aged 9**
**St. Catherine's Prep School, Bramley, Surrey**

# Mystery in the Night

by Hannah James

**That night a mysterious tapping on his bedroom window just wouldn't stop; he had to see what it was**. Cautiously, the boy (Joshua) crept across his creaky, wooden floor, over to the window. Slowly and carefully, he pulled back his tattered curtains. The night sky was a dark, mystifying indigo… full of gloomy mist and fog. Above it all hung a large, snow-white moon like a guardian to us all. It all looked extremely magical; however, something caught Joshua's eye that sent a shiver running down his spine as if someone had put freezing ice cubes in his pyjamas. It was a man. He looked ancient: his gnarled face was pale and his arms thin and frail. Blood-piercing eyes scanned the ground. Looking, watching, searching. Finally, he picked up a stone.

*What on Earth was he going to do with a stone?* Joshua thought. He soon found out.

Nimbly, the man threw the tough stone straight towards the window. Petrified, Joshua sprinted towards his bed and under the covers, waiting for his window to smash… but it didn't! All it made was a small tap. Not sure what to expect, Joshua again tiptoed over to the window.

15

The man caught his eye. What cold eyes those were! However, even though Joshua was freaking out by how horrible they were, he stayed put. He was mesmerised. It was almost as if those eyes hid another world inside. A world of death, hatred… and fear.

Suddenly, he started to feel numbness in his legs. Soon he felt it in his arms. Eventually, the whole of him felt weak. A loud thud then rang out through Josh's room: he had collapsed….

After a while, he woke up, taking in his surroundings. He was in a dark, gloomy room – but not alone! Around him were children. Small children, fat children, thin children, tall children. Children with torn clothes, filthy skin and tangled hair. Children who were dead, children who were still just living.

Instantly, thoughts buzzed around Josh's head like bees attacking a vicious intruder. Was this what he would look like soon if he didn't escape? How did he get here? And who were all these children? He decided to ask one of them. Scanning the room for someone to talk to, Josh felt scared. When he spotted a young girl, he went over to her. Looking into her deep, emotional eyes, he whispered something. 'Hello…' he said.

No answer. He waited. Soon she had the courage to speak. 'Who are you? I have not seen you before,' she asked.

'I'm Josh. I was just wondering, could you tell me where I am?'

'Away from kindness, next to hatred,' she replied.

These words made no sense to Josh, so he decided to take small steps instead. 'What is your name?'

'Sasha,' she mumbled. 'Sasha.' She said it as if it was a foreign word, puzzled over what it meant.

'How did you get here?' wondered Josh.

Sasha sighed. 'I was born here… and soon I will die here.'

These words struck Josh in the face like a slap. He needed to help these children… but how?

**Hannah James, aged 11**
**Heatherside Junior School, Fleet, Hampshire**

17

# Lord of the Ring Doughnuts

(with apologies to JRR Tolkien)

by Daniel Knuckle

**That night a mysterious tapping on his bedroom window just wouldn't stop; he had to see what it was.** As he opened the curtain he was nearly blown five feet across the room. It was a magic time-changing flying carpet.

'Whohow!' said Fred... 'Bob, wake up!'

'Shut your cakehole, Fred. I'm asleep,' but then Bob saw the flying carpet and fell out of his bunk. 'Ow!'

'Come on, let's get on!' Fred cried, excitedly.

'Have you lost your tiny mind? We might miss breakfast....'

But Fred had already dragged his brother onto the carpet. In one, maybe two seconds the carpet had wrapped them up and taken them 3000 years back in time.

They found themselves in a place like a vast vegetable patch. Then Bob saw a wizard. 'Hello, Gandalf,' he said.

'My name is Banana Beard, not Gandalf. You must be Bob and Fred.'

'How did you know?' Bob was confused.

'He's a wizard,' whispered Fred.

They walked to what should have been Fred and Bob's Uncle Elbow's house, he wasn't there, but there was a ring doughnut on the table. There was no time to investigate because Banana Beard was telling Fred and Bob their task: to destroy the Ring Doughnut (with Icing). First, they had to take it to Pastadell where there would be a council meeting.

So, they set off. Unfortunately Bob insisted on carrying all the pans and cooking equipment. After climbing up waterfalls and forest tracks they ran into a man called Applegorn, who agreed to guide them to Pastadell. They finally arrived, and at midday the council meeting started and the Fellowship of the Ring Doughnut was appointed: Applegorn; Legospoon, archer of the Broccoli Forest; Runnerbean, Captain of Gumjaw; Griddle, son of the king of the dwarves; and Banana Beard himself, along with the two brothers Fred and Bob.

The journey began, but they had to turn off their mountain path, because the evil wizard Graterman was throwing avalanches, so they took another way through the middle of the mountain. In there they met lots of scary scoops (these scoops were creatures made from yoghurt and clotted cream). They fought their way through, but Banana Beard was lost to a tomato ketchup monster. Once through the mountain they were attacked in the enchanted Broccoli Forest. Runnerbean was killed by the scoops firing asparagus arrows through his heart. Fred and Bob had to escape.

They rowed to another mountain, along a river. They found they had been going around in circles and decided to have a rest. While they were asleep a creature called Bolus tried to get the Ring Doughnut from them, because he was magnetically affected by it, as were most other creatures. Fred and Bob tied Bolus to a rope and made him lead them to the Mountain of Dough in Mouldor where the Volcano of Hot Batter was, in which the Ring Doughnut (with Icing) could at last be destroyed.

Meanwhile Griddle, Legospoon and Applegorn rode to the land of Roham, where they found King Fishoden trying to lead his people to safety at Porridge Deep, because they were outnumbered by 9000 scoops against only 300 men. As Legospoon and Applegorn were having a heated discussion, they heard a loud horn (that sounded like a huge fart). Legospoon cried, 'Elves! Come on!'

They saw an army of elves, looking like ancient Egyptians, marching towards them. The commander of the elves reached them. Applegorn told him they were most welcome. 'But how did you know we needed help?'

'The Sultan of Pastadell phoned us, (no, sorry, phones aren't invented yet...) he had a magical talk with the Sultan of the Broccoli Forest.'

There was no more time for talking, the scoops were approaching: 'All elves and men to the wall!' cried Lord Applegorn.

As they came closer he shouted, 'Release asparagus!'

The scoops were falling like skittles, but there were too many to hold back. Applegorn cried, 'Raise pizzas! Draw French sticks!'

The battle raged on, until there were only five men left defending the ramparts. Applegorn ordered everyone onto horseback. Suddenly the doors opened, the scoops nearly got in, but the riders trampled them in their suicide charge. Just outside the gates, as they were still fighting for their lives, Banana Beard appeared on the horizon, with 2000 more riders. He had come back to life, with a purple face! When all the scoops were deaded, Banana Beard announced: 'The Food Fight of Porridge Deep is over. The Food Fight of Middle Earth is about to begin.'

Meanwhile, Bolus had led Fred and Bob into Mouldor. Bolus was a very ugly creature, with a bald head, and grey skin, and just a dirty leaf wrapped around his bottom. As they were climbing up the Mountain of Dough, towards the Volcano of Hot Batter, Bolus let out a cry, clutching for the doughnut, which was around Fred's neck. Bob fought him off with a frying pan. They carried on climbing slowly up the Rocky Road.

Banana Beard knew that Graterman

was still creating more scoop armies to take over Middle Earth. He summoned Applegorn, Legospoon and Griddle to lead all the remaining troops towards Mouldor, through the land of Gumjaw. In Gumjaw they got intercepted by a million scoops, and the final battle for Middle Earth began. Graterman released a fountain of melted chocolate over the land. The people of Gumjaw had to slurp for their lives. The land was littered with dead scoops and riders. Things were looking hopeless, then Applegorn appeared with a massive army of indestructible green jelly men, who bounced across the battlefield, squelching the scoops into oblivion.

Graterman was totally distracted by the scene, while behind him Fred and Bob were struggling up the Mountain of Dough. At last they were looking down into the Volcano of Hot Batter, bubbling and spitting below them. Fred cried, 'Let's toss it into the batter!' but Bob just wanted to taste it before it was destroyed. Bob tried to take a bite, but cried out in agony, his teeth were on fire; all he could stammer was,

'Doughnut... doughnut... doughnut....'

Fred snatched the doughnut from Bob, then suddenly Bolus leapt from behind them and grabbed it, knocking Fred backwards into Bob. Fred and Bob fell down the hill, Bolus fell into the batter.

The doughnut was gone, the battle was won. They all lived happily ever after....

The flying carpet swooped down, wrapped them up and hurled them back through their bedroom window. Then they heard Mum calling, 'Come on down, Fred, Bob, or I'll whack you with my rolling pin. Your breakfast pancakes are going cold!'

Bob looked glum.

'Whatever's the matter?' asked Fred.

'I think I ate too many weapons,' he moaned.

**Daniel Knuckle, aged 9**
**Horsley C of E Primary School, Gloucestershire**

**'Ouch! I felt a sharp jab in the ribs. But when I turned round, there was no one there.'**

Francesca Simon

# Raspberry The Red Cat

by Amy Penrose

**Ouch! I felt a sharp jab in the ribs. But when I turned round, there was no one there.**

It was then that I first discovered that my cat, Blueberry, could speak! He said to me, 'There is a mouse with knitting needles in your pocket.'

I was too amazed that he could talk to think about what he said. Then my brain got into action. *A mouse in my pocket, with knitting needles?* I thought. But when I reached in, sure enough, a mouse was right there in my hand.

'Thanks,' it said to me, then it started to unravel my jumper.

'Excuse me,' I said, 'this is the jumper my grandma made me!'

'I'm so sorry but your cat Blueberry, a long time ago, said I had to make him a new blanket if he let me live any longer, and it had to be red.'

Well, I was stuck. I did not want to lose my jumper, but I did not want this little mouse to die. So I said, 'Little mouse, why don't you just buy some wool from the shop?'

'Well your jumper is a very rare colour and there was no wool like it in the shop,' replied the mouse. 'It's made from the juice of a raspberry and the fur of a magnolia bud.'

Then I had a great idea. 'I know, why don't we go to my grandma's house and ask her to make you some wool.'

When the little mouse and I got to my grandma's house we asked her, 'Can you make us some more of this wool?'

'Yes, but you will have to go and get me two raspberries and three magnolia buds,' said Grandma.

So off we went to search in Grandma's garden. It wasn't as easy as we thought. There were many different berries but not the ones we were looking for. We nearly gave up but just then we discovered some raspberries behind the shed, and when we looked up we found a magnolia bush. Grandma asked the farmer at the end of the road for some wool and we put it in a pot with our ingredients to dye it just the right shade of red.

The next day, Granny showed us how to spin it.

'Thank you so much,' said the little mouse. After that she worked for ages knitting a blanket so fine that it was fit for a king. The mouse finally gave Blueberry his new blanket. He immediately snuggled down on it, thanking her with every roll. But when he got up he had turned red!

'Don't worry,' I laughed, 'that dye will wash out easily.'

'No baths,' said Blueberry.

'I'm gonna have to call you Raspberry now!'

said the little mouse.

'OK, joke's over now,' my cat said. 'I'm staying red, no baths for me!'

**Amy Penrose, aged 8**
**The Abbey Junior School, Reading, Berkshire**

# My Father

by Christopher Barnes

**Ouch! I felt a sharp jab in the ribs. But when I turned round, no one was there.** I saw an odd shaped shadow pinned to the dusty floor, but wait, there was no light at all so how could there possibly be a shadow there? I stood in shock for seconds, unable to move, when an old man, wearing nothing but a pair of socks, leapt out from behind a rusty dustbin. I backed away as he came closer, but he eventually reached me and as he did, he whispered my dad's dying words to me... 'Don't forget me.'

I fainted. I don't know how long I was out for, but I woke up in hospital with a sore head and a bruise the size of a football!

It was no dream about the scary man so I was extremely puzzled. As soon as I was allowed out of hospital I went in search for this naked man! I went back to the place where he had appeared but nobody was there. Finally I went home, grabbed a packet of crisps, threw myself onto the sofa and flicked on the TV. An old man, wearing a funny hat, was reporting the mysterious death of someone. I wasn't paying much attention till the same scary man walked behind the reporter, in the background. I suddenly sat up and stared at the TV. This was my chance. I popped my shoes on and dashed to the scene! I had eventually found the naked, wrinkly man!

I stood on the spot, twirling around, looking for the scary dude, when I heard a dramatic scream coming from a gift shop behind me. I ran towards the shop. A breathless lady ran out screaming as if it was the only thing she knew how to do. Then... HE walked out, the scary, naked man. He was carrying a ring as if it was his soul. He came towards me, then passed me. I looked over at him and he winked at me. I was furious.

I quickly ran towards him and asked him what he wanted. He explained that he had died ten years ago in a major car accident. He had been sent to Hell but was so angry and vicious when he got there that even Hell wouldn't let him in; it spat him back up. He had been trapped in the darkness for ten years, waiting for an opportunity to explain things and put things right. Now he was in search of his child, a son he had never seen or cared for before, until now. He thought that if he and his son could be reconciled, and his son could forgive him, he would speak highly of him in his prayers. Then God might rescue him from the darkness and let him into Heaven before it was too late. I couldn't help but feel sorry for him. Then he handed me the ring, he said it was a ring that controlled your mind so you could achieve anything you wanted. He put it on the third finger of my left hand.

I looked at him puzzled, then lost my trail of thought. 'What is your name?' I asked.

'Patrick,' he replied. He disappeared. I was dazzled, I looked around again, but after a while gave this up.

Slowly and tiredly I dragged myself home. I remembered he was searching for his wife and child. I'd never known my dad, but that wasn't him. I went and asked Mom, who was doing the ironing, what Dad's name was. 'Patrick,' she said.

I was shocked! I ran screaming into my bedroom and sat on the window sill. I looked at the ring that Patrick had placed on my finger. *So I can wish for anything?* I thought.

'I will control myself to achieve my wish,' I said to myself quietly. OK... I took a deep breath. I knew what I wanted; it was the same thing that I had wanted all my life. 'I wish to know who my dad is!'

I was awakened from my daydream by the sound of several dogs barking. I jumped down from my window sill and hurtled downstairs towards the door. Outside I found the dogs sitting at the bottom of my drive, as though waiting for me. As I opened the door they stood up, checked I was watching and raced off towards the abandoned train station. I was curious, so I quickly ran after them. After a few minutes I stopped for some air, then carried on running till the dogs stopped and started barking at a bin, the same bin that Patrick had jumped out from.

'BANG!'

I quickly turned around to see where the noise had come from, the dogs had disappeared! Then, there he was... Patrick. I wondered what he was doing here, when it crossed my mind that he may even live here. He walked purposefully towards me. 'H… h… hello,' I said to him.

He answered, 'Hi son.'

I was puzzled. This was the guy from the bin, the guy who had scared me, the guy I had only known for about a month and now he calls me... son. He placed his hand on my shoulder. Suddenly, I started to glow and felt my feet leave the ground. I was hovering right next to him. The ring started to change colour, flew off my finger and spun around quickly. The ring was glowing brightly now.

'Well done, son,' Patrick said to me. 'You have been granted your wish.'

'S... So you are my d... dad?' I asked quietly.

Patrick coughed... cleared his throat and hung his head. 'Yes,' he said.

The ring popped and disappeared, at the same time I fell to the floor and stopped glowing.

'So... Dad,' I said as I took out my mobile phone. 'Shall I call Mom?'

I don't know why I asked that question, because I was already dialling her number. She answered quickly, she must have known it was me. 'Hey Mom... You know Dad?' I said.

'Yeah,' she replied puzzled.

'Well he is standing next to me and I want him to come home now. Please can he come home?' I asked.

There was no answer, just silence, then a beeping noise... Mom had hung up.

'Come on Patr... I mean Dad, let's walk home.'

He followed me along the side streets until we reached No. 11. I rang the door bell and Mom answered. She took one look at Dad and she burst into tears. She ran outside and into his arms, gave him a hug and said to him, 'Is it really you Patrick? What is going on? I saw your body, you died in that car accident! So how can you be...?'

She started crying again. He put his arms around Mom.

'Come in, get some clothes on,' she said. 'Have a shower and a good meal, then you and Jimmy can explain everything.'

Afterwards we sat like a proper family, at the table, and explained everything to Mom. She had so many questions, but we needed to sort out how to get Dad up to Heaven. He told me that it wasn't to do with helping him get... up there, but more about earning his son's love and respect. He had never had the chance to get to know me, as he had died in the car on the way to hospital. He was rushing to get there because I had been born early. My Dad had died on the day I was born and now he was sitting next to me on the sofa. Tears came to my eyes.

'So how long are you here for?' I asked, not knowing how close I was to losing him again.

'I'm not sure son,' he replied.

'But I need you. I want you to stay here with me, Dad,' I sobbed. 'I want to remember you, Dad, forever. Dad... I love... you.' I ran upstairs, the tears streaming down my face. Dad ran up after me. I sat on my window sill again, Dad walked in.

'Hey son... just saying this because now you know me and love me, my time is up and I will probably disappear in a few seconds so... bye, I love you and thanks son!'

I jumped off my window sill and hugged my dad with meaning, tears rolling down my cheeks. Mom was at my bedroom door looking at me, hugging my new dad.

'Bye... Dad!' I cried. Then he disintegrated. I fell to my knees and hung my head... 'Bye Dad!'

Mom ran towards me and held me in her arms. After a few minutes when I had pulled myself together, I got out my best suit for my dad's memorial service – after all it had been ten years tomorrow since we had lost him for the first time.

My nan, my two granddads and family friends were all there at the church to recall their memories. They hadn't a clue what had happened to me in the past month, so a smile did creep across my face as we sang his favourite songs. It was all very sad, but at least I had got to know him briefly, even if he had died on my birthday. I could say I knew my dad and I spoke very highly of him, even though the first time I had seen him he was naked behind a bin at seven o'clock in the evening! At the end of the service I gave a short speech that soon became longer; it was all about how and why I loved my dad in so many ways. I did love my dad, more than my pets, more than my friends and more than any special toy or gift.

In the few hours we had been at my house I had a picture taken with him which now hangs on my wall, so every night I can see his face and see how much he loved me.

As I lay in bed that night a smile turned into a grin and as I gazed at the photo of us, my eyes noticed the time on the clock – midnight. 'Happy Birthday Jimmy,' I said to myself.

**Christopher Barnes, aged 10**
**Woodfield Middle School,**
**Redditch, Worcestershire**

# Who Poked Me?

by Maia Lambert

**Ouch! I felt a sharp jab in the ribs. But when I turned round, no one was there.** I felt cross and cross enough. I ran into my house and told my mum. My mum didn't know what happened. 'Mmmmmmmmm,' she thought aloud and then said, 'Time for tea. And pardon me, where's your brother?'

I wondered if it was my brother who poked me and when I turned around I found my brother laughing in the corner.

'Why are you laughing?' I asked.

He giggled, 'Someone just tickled me and I don't know who because I didn't see them.'

I told him what had happened to me. We were both confused. Then Mum turned the telly on, and we heard on the news that there was a scary, long-armed monster escaped. I looked at my brother and said, 'Maybe it was the long-armed monster that poked and tickled us!'

We went to get our bikes out of the garage. But we didn't find our bikes we found a scary-looking long-armed monster instead.

We were going to run away when the monster said, 'Please don't run. Everyone thinks

I am scary but I want people to like me.'

I looked at my brother and said, 'Well we don't like being poked and tickled very much. That is not how to get friends.'

The monster looked sad. 'How do you get friends then?'

We said, 'You need to help people and not be annoying really.'

'Oh that sounds hard,' said the monster.

Just then we heard some screams. We ran outside and our neighbour's cat was stuck in their tree and was falling down. The long-armed monster stuck out one of his long arms from the garage and grabbed the cat by the tummy and put the cat on the grass. He was safe.

Everyone clapped. The firemen clapped who had just come. They asked the long-armed monster to go and work for them helping with things stuck high up. The long-armed monster was happy. He said to us, 'I promise not to tickle or poke again.'

Then he winked at me and my brother.

**Maia Lambert, aged 6**
**Herstmonceux CE Primary School, East Sussex**

# Who's There?

by Louisa Ashdown

**Ouch! I felt a sharp jab in the ribs. But when I turned round no one was there.** I crept into the kitchen and it was dark. I heard some rustling and I switched the light on. I looked around but there was still nobody there. I could hear horrible panting.

The noise was behind the utility room door. What could it be? A crocodile? A bear? A tiger?

I looked behind the door and it was only Daddy!

**Louisa Ashdown, aged 5**
**The Abbey Junior School, Reading, Berkshire**

'Gary's favourite helmet didn't fit any more and he knew exactly why.'

Oliver Jeffers

# Down the Hole

by Jasmine Thirkell

**Gary's favourite helmet didn't fit any more and he knew exactly why.**

* * *

'Gary, James is at the door wanting to know if you can come and play. Do you want to?' called his mum.

'Yes I will be right down,' he shouted back. So Gary put down his favourite helmet and rushed downstairs to join James. 'Bye Mum,' he called as he walked out the door.

'So where are we going today?' asked Gary, as him and James walked up the drive.

'I thought we could go and check out those woods we saw the other day,' James replied, a huge grin spreading across his face.

'OK, I bet I can beat you there,' boasted Gary.

'You're on,' said James. So off they went, speeding along the pavements and through fields. When they finally got there, James turned to Gary. 'Ha! I beat you!' he screamed in Gary's face. Normally Gary would have tried to prove James wrong at this point, but he was too busy staring at a patch of flowers. 'What's up?' asked James.

'Look,' he replied. 'That patch of flowers, it seems to be sparkling.'

As they started to creep closer, neither of them dared to speak, but then Gary did. 'Look at that, it seems to be a shimmering pool of water.'

As they got closer and closer, James tripped, taking Gary with him. Down and down the hole they fell, and then landed with a thud! They looked up and saw strange people staring at them. All was silent. Then the smallest one said, 'Mummy, Mummy, the prophecy, it's come true. The strangers are here to save us.'

'Take them to our king,' shouted another.

Then the people started carrying them slowly across the town. Then they were put onto a platform where a huge man sat.

'People here to save us at last!' he bellowed. 'All you have to do is go through those gates and there you will find a monster. All you have to do is stare into its eyes.'

'What monster?' Gary trembled, 'and if it is that simple, why don't you do it yourself?'

'The monster is called Gilbert and the legend states nobody from the Underworld can kill it, they got to be from up top.'

'OK we will do it, how hard can it be?' replied James.

Then the people started to lift them, but this time they were put onto the floor and a tall man unlocked the gates and in they went.

'Here we go,' said Gary. Then they met the monster. 'So all we have to do is stare into his eyes, right?' asked Gary.

'Well, that's what he said,' replied James.

So that's what they did and the monster fell to the ground, not breathing or moving a muscle. So they walked back to the gates, smiling, 'We've done it!' and everyone cheered.

This time they walked back to the king, who congratulated them. 'You have done it, you've killed the monster,' he said in a rather loud voice. 'You must join my tribe.'

Then all of a sudden, around eight people, with big ears and large heads, appeared out of nowhere, beside the king. So the two boys climbed up onto the stage to join them. After a couple of hours of fun and games, Gary remembered that they needed to go home, so he told James and they went to speak to the king.

'Excuse me sir, I am sorry to say, but we need to go home. Is there any way out?' they asked.

'Yes, if you stand where you came in and say 'CZAM, CZOOM', then turn around three times, you should be back up top.'

'OK thanks.'

So off they went, did what they needed to do and went back to Gary's house. When they got back, Gary picked up his favourite helmet and tried to put it on his head, but it was too small.

Gary turned to James and screamed,

'AAAAAHHH, James, your ears are huge!'

'Gosh,' James replied, 'your head is massive!'

What had happened had happened down the hole. They had turned into the king's official tribe.

* * *

That's why Gary's favourite helmet doesn't fit any more!

**Jasmine Thirkell, aged 9**
**Hunloke Park Primary School, Derbyshire**

# Oh No, My Helmet!

by Greg Susevee

**Gary's favourite helmet didn't fit any more and he knew exactly why**. Even without trying it on. He would not be able to wear it for some time. Perhaps later on in the year he could wear it again. However, for the next few weeks it would not fit him. He would have to use his spare helmet which was not his favourite but it would have to do.

He put it on, got out his bike and cycled to the shops. Earlier, Gary had been busy gardening in the morning and he had wanted a cool drink. When he opened the fridge, he realised he was out of drinks.

Gary had decided that he would cycle to his local shop to buy some fresh, organic orange juice. This always refreshed him. He had walked to the garden shed to put on his helmet ready for his cycle ride. But there was a problem! This was the moment when Gary had realised that his helmet didn't fit any more, but he did know exactly why!

The cycle ride was relaxing and when he got home he poured himself some juice, took out a cake and sat in the garden to enjoy it. What a lovely tea it was!

'Now, what am I to do about my favourite

helmet? What a funny situation this is. Well I never!' Gary laughed. 'This has never happened before. That is why nature is so wonderful, because it gives so many surprises.' Gary often talked to his dog, Yo-Yo, the German Shepherd.

'I know, old boy, let us dig some soil and find some worms. It might help the parents to build up their strength.'

Gary got his spade and started to dig. He collected a good handful of wonderful wriggling worms and took them towards the garden shed. The worms were scattered on the path near the shed and Gary then stood back to watch.

Within a minute a robin flew down and took a worm whilst singing sweetly. The robin flew to his nest and fed the worm to his mate. She could not get her own food because she was looking after their eggs. The female robin gobbled the worm hungrily. All of a sudden she moved! What was happening? Gary was amazed as he peered through the window of the shed. The eggs were hatching. He was so happy and so excited. Soon there would be baby robins, safe and warm, nesting in his favourite helmet!!!

Robins often nest in unusual places but a cycling helmet! Gary still could not believe his luck. Over the next few weeks he saw the baby robins turn from blind, bald chicks, to brown balls of chirping fluff. He put out plenty of mealworms to feed the male, female and baby robins and he always shooed the neighbour's cat away.

Then one day, Gary noticed that the male and female robins were sat together on the fence, singing so sweetly and loudly. He wondered why they were not looking after their babies. He watched them intently, hoping that the chicks were safe. He thought about going to have a look but he was worried about frightening them, especially as the parents were nearby on the fence.

Soon, his patience was rewarded. The fledglings were about to leave the nest. Out they came – one, two, three, four, five – six little robins, safe and well. Gary was so happy to have helped this little family of robins. However, he knew that robins often had two broods in a year. His thoughts now turned to his helmet. Before they nested again, Gary would have to make some preparations.

When they had all flown from the nest, Gary took the nest from his favourite helmet, which was then cleaned. Although the whole adventure had been exciting, he was glad to have his favourite helmet back again!

'Come on Yo-Yo,' Gary said to his dog. 'Let's go and buy a bird box.'

Gary and Yo-Yo set off to a friend's house. His friend, Peter, was a carpenter and made bird, bug and hedgehog boxes as a hobby. Gary bought a robin bird box and took it home.

He hung it inside his garden shed in the hope that his two robins would come back to his shed to nest again. Next time, he hoped that they would nest in the box and not in his favourite helmet. But he knew robins better than that! Next time, they would probably nest in a drawer! He would learn his lesson and put his favourite helmet away in a 'safe' place!!!

**Greg Susevee, aged 9**
**Awliscombe Primary School, Devon**

**'From a distance, Melton Chipsbury looked like any other quiet country village.'**

Stewart Ross

# The Bookseller

by Harry Carter

**From a distance, Melton Chipsbury looked like
any other quiet country village**, but look closer
and you will find it has a dark history....

It was 6:40 in the morning, and, as usual for
winter weather, it was raining. Hunter lived with
his mum and dad in a one-storey house in Melton
Chipsbury. Deciding that there was nothing else to
do until his parents woke up, he killed the hours
by playing with the wrestling game on his Xbox.

'Yes! Hulk Hogan wins again!' His words
were heard all over the bungalow. Hunter lay
down and stared at his Star Wars poster. He had
always wished that he could be involved in an
adventure like that.

'Are we there yet?'

'No.'

'Come on, I want to get him a book.'

Hunter was conversing with his mum in her
sleek Jaguar about getting Mike, his best friend, a
book from the shop on the other side of town. He
had known Mike since pre-school and they had
first met by playing football together. Just then,
out of the corner of his eye, Hunter saw a strange

hexagonal sign, which read: 'DON'T OPEN THE BOOK!'

What made it even more strange was that on the other side of the blackout windows was the same message, but graffitied on the wall. He rubbed his eyes.

'What's the matter dear?' his mum enquired.

'Ummm… nothing. It's nothing…' he answered.

He tried to forget about the strange message to put his mind at ease.

Hunter was surrounded. Surrounded by thousands of leather-bound books. He had never seen so many. From amphibians to Zeus, the shop had it all.

'Can I help you, sir?'

Hunter turned round to face an old gentleman of around 65. He was dressed in a dirty suit with a brown sweater under the jacket.

'Yes, please,' he replied, 'I'm looking for a book for my friend….'

'Ah… I have just the book you're looking for!' The old man's eyes gleamed. With some difficulty, he raised himself from behind his oak desk and led Hunter towards a shelf at the back of the shop. 'I remember a long time ago, a boy your age came looking for a book…' began the old man, putting on his glasses. He peered at the bookcase and pulled down a battered-looking book with a tatty paper cover and torn spine. 'Ah, here it is. This is the one: a book full of real adventure.'

As the old man passed him the book, Hunter felt a strange shiver come over him. It was then that he remembered the sign and the warning in graffiti. An urge to open the book crept into Hunter's thoughts but a feeling to throw it away tried to take control. He was stuck in a dilemma.

'What's it about?' questioned Hunter, eagerly.

'Oh, wonderful things!' The man's eyes gleamed.

Hunter opened the book...

WAAAAAAHH! Hunter's ears rang as a sudden sound exploded behind him. 'What?'

Kaboom! Something shattered.

Hunter had watched enough films to know he was in a warzone – but how? The book! It must have transported him but this was like no place he had seen before. There were no trees, no plants and no humans. He could just make out cannons filled with fire and monsters with axes chopping down their foes. He started to run as fast as he could. Two armies were charging at each other and Hunter was caught in the middle of it. He saw them fall to the ground with bullets in their chests. He had loved the films but now he realised that someone's life was taken with every shot. It did not matter what they looked like, they all had a life. Orc-like beings were stumbling around, bumping into each other and firing aimlessly at their elfish foes.

He came to a rock. Not an ordinary rock, but one the size of a house and at the front of it was a huge hole with an arched entrance. Peering through the swirling mist that seeped from the archway, Hunter could just make out an old man with his back to him, wearing long, colourless robes.

HUMMMM. A droning noise surrounded the old man. He seemed to be in a trance of some sort, so Hunter crept into the cave and looked around cautiously. There were strange objects hanging from the wall, such as bronze dragons encrusted with gold, silver, crystal, emerald, ruby, sapphire, pearl, diamond and every other rare stone. Hunter was surprised that a place so strange yet calm could be next to a warzone. In the corner of the room was a single cabinet with an old book on the top. It looked just like the volume that had transported him here! He was just about to lift it when, for some reason, he turned around. What he saw sent a shiver down his spine: the man was levitating in midair with no supports.

'Ahh...' he whispered peacefully, 'you want book?' He slowly opened his eyes and they were gleaming.

'Umm... will it take...?'

The man interrupted him: 'Yes.'

Hunter could still hear the repulsive bombshells destroying the ground. 'What's all this fighting?'

The old man answered, 'It was orcs. They destroy villages. I am last of family.'

The boy noticed how his English was not fluent but also that, to his horror, an eye on the man's forehead blinked every minute. 'You want go back?'

'Yes, I....'

'Do you like here?' he interrupted again.

Hunter started to wonder why he was even asking the questions if he was just going to break in every sentence halfway through.'Not at all!'

The old man floated down to the ground and picked up the book. 'Here, keep.'

Just like last time, when Hunter was about to open the book, he got the feeling again: should he do it or not?

'Thank you,' Hunter told the man and, taking one last glimpse of the room he heard one last gunshot as he tore open the pages.

'What do you think? I told you... real adventure!' He was back in the shop. The old bookseller's eyes gleamed.

**Harry Carter, aged 10**
**West Leigh Junior School, Leigh-on-Sea, Essex**

# Behind the Sign

by Georgina Evans

**From a distance, Melton Chipsbury looked like any other quiet country village.** Great! Just what I needed! A boring, empty, full-of-bookshops-and-souvenir-shops area. Of course, it has NO kids playground, NO toyshops, NO swimming pool and NO rocks to climb! How more unlively can it get, I'd like to know? Not much worse than this... yet Scott had a look of absolute awe warming up his chilled, pale face. It was FREEZING in our old orange camper van. Dad told me it was all part of the experience. I mumbled about the other part being trapped in a stupid village called Melton Chipsbury.

When we arrived, the owner of the caravan park showed us to the spot we were supposed to be in. I noticed his teeth were yellow.

'We don' get many people round 'ere nowadays,' he boomed, picking dirt off his thumbnails. 'But ya'll enjoy it, promise. No spiders or mice. Nuffink at all.'

As I was on my holiday with my mum and dad, I'd been allowed to choose one friend to take with me. I didn't need telling twice. Scott came along too.

When we were all settled we headed into the town. It was a small but cosy place. The very first shop I bounded into was an ancient sweet shop through an alleyway, next to a woolly jumper shop.

'The Oldest Sweet Shop in the World' it read in huge gold writing. Perfect for me! I'd always been one for buying delicious and nutritious sweets and choccies. I stepped into the tiny building and breathed in a lovely sugary scent. It was a small but neat area. There were glass jars smothering the pale lilac walls. I noticed a sign saying 'Jelly babies coming soon' in the far corner of the wall. I gazed longingly around the room. It was remarkable. There were: apple shoelaces, chocolate buttons, chocolate oranges, toothbrushes, dummies, milk and cola bottles, eggs, teddy bears, jelly rings, sugar bracelets, Rowntree's trucks, traffic light lollipops, jelly spiders, sugar mice, teeth and lips, eyeball gum, jelly hearts and fizzy body parts.

Across the other side of the safe room there was a set of spiral stairs. But there was obviously something wrong because there was a huge DANGER sign, like the kind you find if you're stood in front of a 500-foot drop.

I pondered over what was upstairs. Could it be a giant, three-headed dog? Or maybe a half man, half horse, complete with a bow and arrow?

'Dolly?' Scott mumbled as he peered over the top of his book, 'The World Of Insects', and sucked on a toffee. It was time to leave. I shuffled slowly out of the shop, hearing the alarming doorbell cry behind me.

I was determined to find out what was up there, sign or no sign. I told Scott that evening. His eyes were glued to the same book as before. I sighed deeply. He'd always been a clever goody-two-shoes. I was much more interested in climbing and getting into trouble. I knew that if I wanted to see what was up there then I had to do it fast because we were only at Melton Chipsbury for three days.

The next morning, I shook Scott awake extremely early, whispering to him to get dressed quickly.

'Dad, me and Scott are gonna head into town. We'll see you back here in about an hour.' Well, that's what I thought then.

We thundered down the empty street and turned left to a narrow, cobbled lane. The sweet shop was second on the right. I was so excited; I nearly walked straight past it.

Anyway, we arrived at the mysterious place and I heard the familiar *DING-DONG* of the rusty doorbell. It sounded like an angel singing, it was so high and soft. I nodded slightly at Scott, knowing the shopkeeper (or the body woman, as they called her) would be watching our every move. Scott knew that the nod meant to get started on our cunning tricks.

I shuffled slowly to the far corner of the

shop, pretending to be looking for a sweet that took my fancy. Scott sneezed loudly (well, at least *pretended* to) and the body woman glanced in his direction. That was my chance! One size-three foot darted forwards, my dirty hand dived out and, SMASH! A jar quite far away from me shattered, scattering me with tiny shards of glass. I leapt away, acting 'being shocked'. As the body woman slumped lazily behind the counter to the back part of the shop to collect a dustpan and brush, her beady green eyes left Scott and I alone. At last! Scott pulled open the door slightly so that the bell chimed and the body woman thought we'd left. She was SO wrong! We sped up the creaky stairs, going so fast that they didn't creak at all.

Finally we were up in the place that every single resident of Melton Chipsbury wanted to be. We were in the attic of the oldest sweet shop in the world. I breathed in the musty smell and shut my eyes tight, hardly daring to believe what we'd done or where we were.

Starting to get excited, I peered inside one of the boxes labelled 'Jelly Spiders'... and instead of what any normal person would expect; the sweet version of spiders – thousands of tiny black dots were scuttling up and down my arms, now with goose bumps on them. I had to press my pale lips together to prevent a loud scream leaking out.

Shaking the minute insects off my skinny arms, I crossed carefully to another box and hovered over it.

'Dolly?' Scott called out softly. 'Dolly, what's wrong?'

But I was speechless. My small mouth was moving but Scott couldn't hear my boyish voice. He crossed the small attic and perched down beside me. I heard his breath suck in as he gasped. We were peering in the Jelly Babies box. But there were no sweets there. There were three bawling babies, real life, shouting and crying.

It was too much for me. I don't normally cry but the thought of these cute little babies being turned into sweets was terrible. There was a deafening silence after that and Scott was the first one to break it.

'Let's do it to her,' he whispered. 'Let's turn her into a sweet.'

There was a machine in the corner that was obviously what she used to transform them. It was a magnificent red, with all sorts of unusual contraptions. It was named 'The Sizzler for Sweets' and it was complete with bolts and chains and goodness knows what else.

Abruptly, before we could admire every inch of it, I stumbled noisily over a box of real toothbrushes; that was why the caravan owner's teeth were so mangy, his toothbrush had been stolen! Anyway, it made such a racket that we could hear the distant *STOMP STOMP STOMP* of the body woman's footsteps clacking up the ancient staircase. There was no time to lose.

I was ready and waiting just behind the

creaky door. It opened gradually, groaning louder than ever in the silent, stuffy room. Eventually the door was open wide enough for the body woman to comfortably shuffle through. I hid behind the safety of the door, hardly breathing at all. Then, *THUMP!* I leapt out from behind the wooden door and the body woman realised that I was there. Scott scooted out of the door just before the body woman slammed the door shut and trapped me. Scott was free. I wasn't.

Two days later, a sign appeared outside the shop. 'Dolly Mixtures coming soon.'

**Georgina Evans, aged 10**
**Warley Road Primary School,**
**Halifax, West Yorkshire**

**" 'Head for the hills everybody!' screamed the lookout. 'The Vikings are coming!' "**

Tony Bradman

# Vikings Come to Dublin

by Eleanor Moloney

**'Head for the hills everybody!' screamed the lookout. 'The Vikings are coming!'**

'Get the scrolls out first!' yelled one monk.

'No, the chalices,' shrieked another.

'Someone grab the Book of Kells!' hollered the lookout.

All of the monks grabbed the precious treasures. Everybody heard that the Vikings were coming to Dublin. Everybody except one monk....

Brother Cian (who was a vain and forgetful monk) was supposedly finishing St John's Gospel. He was however listening to 'Bad Boys' by Alexandra Burke on his iPod. The gospel was lying untouched on the chair beside him. Suddenly, his iPhone rang, but Cian did not hear it. This was very strange because Cian was a strong believer that when his phone rang he must answer it. In fact, he was so intent on listening to the song that he had forgotten all his worries. He had forgotten that his computer was broken and that his Nintendo DS needed charging....

Just then the door burst open and Cian's best friend, Brother Paddy, came in. At this moment Cian decided to dance to the music. Some might say his dancing resembled a nutty kung fu expert rather than a groovy monk. Anyhow....

'Cian! The Vikings are coming. Everyone is heading for the hills,' Paddy cried. Cian, who was so engrossed in his dancing, did not hear him but instead began to elbow thin air. Subsequently, Paddy was elbowed in the face. He fell onto his round bottom, his nose bleeding heavily. He struggled to his feet and yanked the headphones out of Cian's ears.

'The Vikings are coming!' Paddy yelled into Cian's ear.

'You don't have to shout,' Cian protested. 'And why is your nose bleeding?'

'Long story,' Paddy said. 'But what's more important is that the Viking longboat has been spotted. Everyone is heading for the hills.'

'Well, why didn't someone tell me?' asked Cian!

**Eleanor Moloney, aged 9**
**Carnaross National School,**
**County Meath, Ireland**

# The Attack of the Vikings

by William O'Hara

**'Head for the hills, everybody!' screamed the
lookout. 'The Vikings are coming!'**
There was pandemonium in the Anglo-
Saxon village of Burntwood. People were rushing
here, there and everywhere: mothers grabbing
children, farmers grabbing livestock and men
preparing their weapons. The sound of the
Vikings' thundering footsteps could be heard
above the terrible screams.

'Hurry up, Aedre!' shouted her husband
Harold, worriedly. 'We don't have much time.
The Vikings will be here soon.'

'I am being as quick as I can,' replied Aedre,
distraught. 'Where is Ace?' She scanned the
chaotic scene, searching for her son. Storm clouds
were gathering overhead, thundering like war
drums. Eventually, she saw Ace running like a
startled hare through the crowd. 'Where have
you been?' she shouted hysterically, tears
drenching her face like rain.

'I was playing in the fields,' explained Ace.
He looked petrified.

'Come on you two. There is no time for this!'
bellowed Harold. He pushed his wife and son out

of the hut. He grabbed a pig and some possessions wrapped up in a bundle. The villagers were pushing and shoving to get to the hills, streaming out of the streets.

'If we get to the hills, we might be able to escape from the Vikings,' said Harold, strangely calm. The sound of the Vikings' crashing footsteps was getting nearer. There was fear on everyone's faces. When they got to the top of the hill they set up camp. Just then Ace realised how high up he was. By now the Vikings were almost on top of them. Out of the crowd appeared an oddly dressed Viking. His voice echoed throughout the hills.

'I am the Viking Warrior Chief, Thor,' he bellowed. 'I have the honour of leading this fleet into battle.'

Tentatively, the chief of the settlement rose. 'I am Abrecan, chief of the settlement,' he said feebly.

'Silence!' roared Thor.

'Yes sir,' he whimpered. You could see his fear, painted like a picture on his face.

'I am taking control of this village. No exceptions,' shouted Thor.

Just then Ace piped up. 'What if we refuse?' said Ace confidently.

'If you and the villagers are stupid enough to refuse, then my men and I, with great satisfaction, shall kill every last pathetic man, woman and child,' laughed Thor.

'Back down,' whispered Aedre, her face full of fear. Ace obeyed his mother and returned to the tent.

'You have five days to submit,' finished Thor. 'If you refuse, my men and I will attack.'

After the conversation the chief of the settlement called a town meeting.

'We can do something!' shouted a woman among the crowd.

'Calm down!' shouted the chief of the settlement. 'We must agree,' he said solemnly.

'No!' bellowed Ace in a surprisingly loud voice. 'We must not give in!'

'You have no say in the matter,' said the chief of the settlement.

Ace stomped away from the meeting angrily. He lay against a large rock, looking at the stars. He stayed there for ages listening to the sound of the gentle breeze. He stretched out his arms and legs. He was very tired from his journey up the hill. Suddenly a small rock disappeared from under his left foot and he fell through a hole in the ground into a large passage. A little shaken, he followed the passage all the way to the end and was amazed at what he saw. He had found an abandoned village. The huts were old, but still standing.

'The village is saved!' he cried. Ace ran back to the village and burst back into the meeting. 'I have found a way to save the village,' he said with a grin on his face. 'You must come!'

'This had better be worth it, Ace,' said the chief of the settlement.

Ace showed everybody how he had found the passage.

'This is excellent,' cried the chief of the settlement. 'Gather your possessions everyone. We are going to be fine.' There were cheers from the crowd of villagers.

Everybody moved into one of the huts. There were plenty to go round. Once everybody had moved in there was a ceremony. 'Ace, you have saved us all,' said the chief of the settlement. 'In honour of your achievement, I present you with the Shield of the Village. When I die, you shall be the next chief of the settlement.'

'Thank you so much sir,' said Ace as he accepted the shield.

Some time later, before the chief died, his final words were of the passage that saved the village. As promised, Ace became the new chief and ruled successfully.

Legend has it that the Vikings never found the village and that the origin of the secret passage was never discovered. However, legend and fact are rarely one and the same....

**William O'Hara, aged 9**
**Brentwood Prep School, Essex**

# The Garbage Monster

'I'm a monster on a mission,
To gobble up your waste...'

Roger McGough

# The Garbage Monster

by Katrina Harris

**I'm a monster on a mission,**
**To gobble up your waste,**
Just chuck something in me,
I don't care about the taste.

I love all the leftovers,
Banana peel is such a treat,
I especially love mouldy fruit,
Old custard and out of date mincemeat.

I'm a monster on a mission,
With a mouth that opens wide,
I speak a load of rubbish,
Because I keep it all inside.

Every home needs one of me,
Without me you'd be stuck,
Your house would be a messy heap,
Of slime and dirt and muck.

I'm a monster on a mission,
I may not be clever, cute or thin,
So don't go and hide me away,
Because I'm only a little bin!

**Katrina Harris, aged 11**
**Robert Gordon's College, Aberdeen**

# The Garbage Monster

by Jake Wood

**I'm a monster on a mission
to gobble up your waste.**
Leave all your bins out tonight
so I can have a taste.
When nighttime comes, I wake up
and come around your house.
You'll be sleeping in your beds
so I'll be as quiet as a mouse.
When you wake up and look outside
your bins will all be clean.
Because I'm the garbage monster,
to help keep our planet green.

**Jake Wood, aged 8
Great Paxton Primary School, Cambridgeshire**

# The Garbage Monster

by Evie O'Neill

**I'm a monster on a mission**
**To gobble up your waste.**
I think you kind of lucky
That I have this type of taste.

To keep the planet healthy
You'll have to be more green.
Recycle all your rubbish
If you want a world that's clean.

Too much food is wasted,
Dumped into the ground.
Yet in other places
There's not enough to go around.

We need to save our energy
Turn the lights off when you're done.
Don't leave things on standby
What a DIFFERENCE for everyone!

We are using too much oil
And soon it will be gone.
Can we not make better use
Of the sea, wind and sun?

So now's the time for change
We just can't carry on.
Small steps will made a difference,
For the sake of EVERYONE!

**Evie O'Neill, aged 10**
**Norwich High School for Girls, Norfolk**